MAKE·BELIEVE
BALL PLAYER

Other Books by Alfred Slote

MAKE·BELIEVE BALL PLAYER

Alfred Slote
Drawings by Tom Newsom

J. B. LIPPINCOTT   NEW YORK

J
Slote

Library of Congress Cataloging-in-Publication Data
Slote, Alfred.
  Make-believe ball player / by Alfred Slote ; drawings by Tom
Newsom.
    p.   cm.
  Summary: Although he's not very good at baseball, ten-year-old
Henry uses his imagination to become a better ball player.
  ISBN 0-397-32285-2 : $. — ISBN 0-397-32286-0 (lib. bdg.) :
$
  [1. Baseball—Fiction.   2. Imagination—Fiction.   3. Self-
confidence—Fiction.]   I. Newsom, Tom, ill.   II. Title.
PZ7.S635Mak 1989   89-30598
[Fic]—dc19   CIP
                                                         AC

To Siggy and Willie,
but definitely not to Beanbelly

MAKE-BELIEVE BALL PLAYER

1

No hitter in there, Smitty," Ted and Mike Kohn shouted from the outfield.

"Buncha bums," Rachel Dotson called in from right.

"No stick, babe," Gary Stillwell said softly from behind his glove at shortstop. Gary was the best ball player on the team next to me. I was the Sampson Park School Tigers' number-one pitcher. Gary was number two. When he pitched, I played short.

On the bench, Mr. Stillwell, Gary's dad, hollered out in his big booming voice: "You got a no-hitter, Smitty. Just pitch away, lad."

"Let 'em hit," Tony Greene said from second, and Ed Godfrey at third just kept repeating: "Smoke 'em, Smitty. Smoke 'em."

I, Henry Smith, starting pitcher for the Sampson Park Tigers, looked in to get the signal from my catcher, Casey Prince. Old Case wiggled one finger and wagged it toward the batter. That meant he was calling for an inside fastball. Joey Marshall, the Lawton School Lions' best hitter, was up. Joe, being a plate crowder, would have a hard time getting around on an inside fastball.

I pushed my glasses back. I didn't want them to fall off when I went to a full windup. I pumped, kicked, and threw inside.

Joey swung. He did not get around on it. It went off the handle of his bat. An easy pop-up right at me.

"I got it," Kevin Kline, our first baseman shouted, running toward the mound.

"Mine," I yelled. I wasn't taking any chances on someone muffing the last out of the game. The ball came down into my glove.

Cheers went up from our sideline, the subs,

parents. Lots of "Way to go, Sampson Park," "Way to go Smitty," were sounding when Mom's voice cut into the shouts of the crowd.

"Henry!"

Silence.

"Would you please stop making that noise while Mrs. Harrington is here."

"Sorry, Mom. I forgot."

It irritated me that she called my make-believe ball games noise. She was angry, because I had promised not to play when she had a customer in the house. Especially a customer like Mrs. Harrington, who was one of the richest people in Arborville.

Mrs. Harrington bought a lot of Mom's Asian folk art. Twice now my mom has gone off to Burma, Thailand, Indonesia, Malaysia, to buy folk art. She goes into little villages and buys sculpture and weavings and pottery and has it shipped back to Michigan, where she sells it to rich ladies like Mrs. Harrington.

I knew she was expecting to sell Mrs. Harrington the five-foot white wooden elephant from Thailand.

My last pitch had hit the mattress and rolled

off into the side garden. I unhooked the mattress and hauled it to the breezeway.

Through the screen door I could hear Mrs. Harrington saying, "What on earth is Henry doing, Emily?"

"Playing make-believe baseball," Mom replied. "The boy has an overheated imagination. He hangs a mattress on the garage and pretends he is all twenty players."

Mrs. Harrington laughed. "Eighteen players, Emily. Nine to a team. But how wonderful for a child to play make-believe anything in these days of television."

"It's not wonderful at all," Mom said crossly. "The sound of that ball hitting the mattress drives me crazy. I keep waiting for the next *boof*. And sometimes the *boof* doesn't come. I relax, and then . . . *boof!*"

I laughed. The reason the *boof* doesn't come in a regular rhythm is because sometimes I try to pick a runner off first or second. But there was no point explaining that to Mom.

Mom went on, "I wouldn't mind so much if Henry would be just the players, but he has to be the coaches and the parents, too. He changes his voice for that. He's only ten years old. I don't think this is normal behavior. It would be a lot more normal if he went to the park and played a real game with real children his own age."

"More normal, perhaps, but not as much fun," Mrs. Harrington said. "Now, Emily, let's talk about that elephant you've been unable to unload."

"Mrs. Harrington," Mom said with horror in her voice, "I have not offered that to anyone. In fact, I have hidden it so you could be the first to see it. I could sell the elephant at the drop of a hat."

"Nonsense. It's too big for anyone's house but mine. Secondly, you know my husband and I are crazy about large animals. Where on earth did you get it?"

"Thailand. In a little village."

"I suppose you want an arm and a leg for it."

"Mrs. Harrington, what would I do with one of your arms or legs?"

Mrs. Harrington laughed. So did I. I could listen to Mom and her customers all day long.

"Well, Emily, what *do* you want for it?"

"My husband will kill me, but I've priced it at only eight hundred dollars."

I grinned. Mom was shameless bringing Dad in like that. Dad couldn't have cared less about her business. He was a surgeon. He worked nights and days at the hospital. Her business amused him. And sometimes irritated him.

Mom used to be a nurse. But after Dad started making money as a doctor, she quit her nursing job and had kids. My sister Melissa and me. Four years ago, when I was in first grade, Mom said she was going back to school to study art.

"I refuse to stay in the house all my life."

"What's wrong with the house?" Dad had said. And then he said something that got both Mom and Melissa mad at him. He sat back and said, "Women, my dear Emily, belong in the house."

"What did you say?" Mom had asked furiously.

So Dad said it again, sitting back in his chair like a king almost. "Women, my dear Emily, belong in the house."

"Well, I don't," Mom had snapped. "I intend to buy and sell Asian folk art."

I don't think Dad thought she'd go through

with it. But she did. When Mom finished her course at the university, she arranged for a housekeeper to take care of us for two weeks. And to Dad's surprise, she arranged a trip for herself to Asia.

Melissa and I were proud of her. Not everyone's mom did something like that. Lots of doctors' wives just play tennis all day. Our mom flies to Asia! But after a while we got to be as annoyed as Dad. Because after she returned, our house started filling up with carved animals, temple posts, puppets, statues, pots, bowls, toys. We have a big house, but suddenly you could hardly move around in it.

Worse, for a while nothing sold. I thought those carved monkeys and tigers would be with us the rest of our lives. Then one day a doctor's wife bought an Indonesian puppet, and then another doctor's wife bought a tiger, and pretty soon Mom was selling things to women who were not married to doctors. The *Arborville News* even ran an article on Mom and her collection. Lots of people started calling and coming around after that.

Mom's been back to Asia again, and once more

our house is crammed with everything from tigers and monkeys to temple bells.

There's so much stuff and it's so expensive that I was forbidden to play my make-believe games inside. That happened because one day after school I was playing a make-believe game called "tooken in the end zone." It was called that by my parents because when I was about four years old I'd put on a football helmet, and holding a tiny plastic football in my hands, I'd say (according to them):

"And the ball is tooken in the end zone by Henry Smith. Smitty is cutting upfield."

After that we always called make-believe football "tooken" for short. Well, I still play tooken. And one day last year I was playing tooken for the Chicago Bears. I had received the kickoff ten yards behind the goal line in the dining room. I ran it back through the dining room, living room, den, for a touchdown, dodging tacklers everywhere. In avoiding one vicious tackle in the front hall, I ran into one of Mom's expensive Chinese vases and it broke into a zillion pieces.

Oh was there shouting and tears! Mom cried.

I cried. That night Dad, tired from seeing patients all day, looked at the broken vase and shook his head.

"Two things are wrong," he said. "There's too much stuff in the house, and Henry, you're too big to play tooken or any make-believe game indoors."

"Do you want me to rent a store, Larry?" Mom asked, knowing Dad did not want her to spend any more money on the art than she already was spending.

"No," he said. "Henry will have to play his crazy games outdoors from now on."

"They're not crazy games and I don't want to play them outside."

"Why not?" Dad said. "It's nice outdoors. There's fresh air outdoors."

"I know why he doesn't want to play outside," my sister Melissa said. She's twelve, two years older than me, and knows everything.

"Why?" Dad asked.

"He's afraid someone will see him and make fun of him. Especially when they hear him pretending to be all those people, making those funny noises."

I could have kicked her. She was right, but she didn't have to say that.

"That's a chance he'll have to take, then," Dad said. He turned to me. "No more make-believe games inside, Henry."

When Dad gave an order, that was that.

I was too chicken to play outside. So for a while I gave up my games. After school I read or watched TV. But then one day this spring I got tired of reading and I went outside.

Baseball season was going to start soon.

No one was around. No neighbors, no one. I went into the breezeway and got out an old mattress that was just sitting there. I hung it from one of the garage-door handles. Then I started pitching to it. I was pitching for the New York Mets. Even though I live in Arborville, Michigan, and like everyone root for the Detroit Tigers, in my make-believe games I always pitch for the Mets or some other National League team. That's because the American League doesn't let the pitchers hit. They have designated hitters. And in my games I often make an important hit as well as pitch.

That day I was pitching for the Mets against the

New York Yankees—it was a World Series game. I had pitched and batted and fielded for two innings before I decided to add sound. At first quiet sound, but as the game got more exciting, I played everyone. Players, coaches, managers, umpires, even the broadcasters.

Of course I would stop when a deliveryman came by or a neighbor. I'd also stop when someone drove by looking for a house number. But I didn't stop when Melissa came home, which was probably a mistake. She watched me for a minute and then shook her head.

"You know what they do with people who talk to themselves?"

"I'm not talking to myself. I'm playing a game."

"They lock them up." She marched into the house.

"No, they don't," I called after her. "They put them on the stage."

I was getting back at her. Melissa wanted to be an actress when she grew up. She was always over at Junior Theater in Sampson Park trying out for a role in some play. I thought acting was baby stuff. A curtain goes up and you start making speeches.

I liked what I did more. It was realer. Also I was beginning to like playing my make-believe ball games in the driveway. It gave me more room than the living room, dining room, kitchen, and den combined. And Mom was so glad to have me out of the house, she even let me draw a home plate on the mattress.

The only rule was: I had to quit when a customer was inside. Like Mrs. Harrington.

After I pushed the mattress back into its spot in the breezeway, I wondered what to do next. It was Saturday. A Saturday in summer can be very boring. A few birds were twittering in the trees, and a yellow butterfly was crisscrossing Mom's flowers.

I could hear some kids shouting at Sampson Park, but I sure wasn't going over there.

The side door opened, and Mom came out looking pleased.

"How is it going?" I asked.

"Mrs. Harrington is buying the elephant."

"Hooray."

"Sshh. Not so loud."

She opened the garage door.

· 13 ·

"What're you doing?"

"I've got to find a carton big enough for it. She wants to sneak it into her house. It's to be a surprise for Mr. Harrington tonight."

"He'll sure be surprised when he finds an elephant in his living room."

"He'll be delighted," Mom said. She started tossing boxes and cartons about.

"Do you want me to help you find a carton?"

"Henry, the best thing you could do for me is to go to the park and find someone your age to play with."

"Nobody my age wants to play with me."

"How do you know that if you don't go and see? Ah, this is big enough."

She found a carton almost as big as she was.

"You can't put the elephant in that and carry it, Mom."

"Your father will help me. Now if you really want to be helpful, neaten up the mess I made and then go and play in the park. Your sister has no problem going to the park."

"She goes inside the theater."

"You can go there too."

"I'm a ball player," I said.

She went back into the house.

I stacked up the cartons. Then I waited around for Mrs. Harrington to leave so I could start playing again. Soon, though, I heard the rattle of teacups.

That was it. Mrs. Harrington was staying for tea. Now there was nothing for me to do but go to the park and hope there was nobody my age there for me to play with.

2

Sampson Park is a great park. The best park in Arborville. It's got ball diamonds, tennis courts, basketball courts, swings and teeter-totters, a wading pool that's open in summer. It has a little hill, soccer fields. And the Junior Theater building near the parking lot.

As I turned onto Baldwin Avenue, I could hear music and shouts from Junior Theater. I could also hear shouts from Diamond One, which isn't far from the theater. There's only the parking lot between them.

As I crossed the parking lot, I heard a drum go bang and someone inside the building shout: "Stand up for the king, young man."

It sounded like Melissa. I didn't hear any other actors' lines, because just then someone on Diamond One shouted: "No stick, Gary."

My heart sank. The Sampson Park Tigers, the kids from my class at Sampson Park School, were playing a game.

Maybe I should go home right now. No, they couldn't ask me to play. I hadn't signed up for this year's team. I was safe.

From the parking lot I had a good view of Diamond One. Sure enough, it was the Tigers. And player for player practically the same team that was in my make-believe game. Without me, of course.

Kevin Kline was at first, Tony Greene at second, Rachel Dotson was at short, Ed Godfrey at third. In the outfield were Mike Kohn in left, Ted Kohn, his twin brother, in center . . . and—there was no one in right field.

I should have had the sense right then and there to turn around and go home. But I wanted to watch. And I didn't think they could see me.

Gary Stillwell was pitching and Casey Prince was catching. Mr. Stillwell was on the bench. He was calling out to Ted Kohn to move more to right.

"You got to cover two fields, Ted," he boomed out.

"Hey, Mr. Stillwell, there's Henry Smith," Rachel said. "He could play right field."

Oh, Rachel.

Kevin Kline turned around. He shook his head. "Rache, we're better off with a tree than with Smith."

I made believe I didn't hear that.

"We'll have to forfeit next inning if we don't get another player," Rachel shot back.

"Time, ump," Mr. Stillwell called. He looked toward me.

Run, a little voice inside me said. Beat it. Scoot!

But I just stood there with my baseball glove. And all the while I could hear the play being rehearsed in the nearby theater.

"Your majesty, I'm here because I think I can make the princess talk."

"Nonsense, Jack," a little high-pitched voice replied, "better men than you have tried. Go home before you lose your life."

"King," said an adult voice (the director's?), "you've got to sound more kingly."

"Henry," Mr. Stillwell said, "we need a ninth

player by the second inning or we default the game. What do you say?"

"Smith'll mess up terrible, Mr. Stillwell," Ed Godfrey said. "Maybe someone else'll come along."

"No one else is gonna come along," Gary said.

The plate umpire intercepted Mr. Stillwell on his way out to me. He was about sixteen years old. "Is he in fifth grade, Coach?" he asked in a high squeaky voice.

"Yeah, he's in our class, Jimmy," Kevin said to the ump. "He was on our team two years ago."

"Henry's still on our team roster, Jim." Mr. Stillwell's voice boomed out even though he was only six feet away from the umpire.

Gary told me once his dad was a construction foreman. I guess he shouted a lot in his business.

"Henry," he shouted at me, "it's time for your comeback, lad. Get over there in right field."

The "comeback" was about how badly I'd played in third grade. I was okay in second grade, when there was no pitching. We hit off a tee then. But in third grade pitching started. And I struck out all the time.

I wasn't much better in the field. I think I caught

only one ball all season. I just don't see very well. Even with strong glasses.

In fourth grade I didn't even go out for the team. Though Mr. Stillwell told me he'd keep me on the roster in case I changed my mind. Which I didn't think I ever would.

"Come on, Henry, we need you," Casey called from behind the bat.

That settled it. If old Case wanted me to play, I would.

"Okay," I said, and tried to look brave. I hustled onto the field.

"Henry Smith's our ninth man, Dick," Mr. Stillwell informed the other coach.

The other coach laughed. "Suits me." He must have remembered me from two years ago.

I squinted to see who the other team was. They had on orange T-shirts. It looked like the Angell School Comets. They were tough.

"Batter up," said the squeaky-voiced ump named Jimmy.

I pounded my glove. I wasn't pounding it as hard as my heart was pounding me.

I took a deep breath. And then to make my

shakes go away, I shouted: "No stick in there, Gary."

Everyone else was yelling, so thank goodness no one heard me.

Gary threw two fastballs for strikes, and then the batter popped up to Kevin Kline at first. He gobbled it up.

"Way to go, Kev," I called out, thinking I probably should have moved in to back him up in case he dropped it. I really didn't have an outfielder's instincts. But right field was always where they put me. That's where the fewest balls are supposed to be hit.

The infield whipped the ball around. I wished Mom could see me now.

I felt a lot calmer when the next batter grounded out to Kevin, who made the play unassisted. Though again I probably should have moved in to back him up. But Kevin didn't miss it. It was all just like my make-believe game. Only it was Gary's fastball they weren't getting around on.

The third batter fouled out to Casey. And we were up to bat.

I ran in. Ted Kohn ran in with me. "They're

not getting around on Gary's fastball," he said.

"I know that," I said, miffed that he felt he had to point that out to me.

"That means you could be getting some business out in right field from right-handed batters swinging late."

"Right," I said, wondering if he was trying to make me nervous.

"Keep on your toes, Henry," Ted said, and slapped me on the arm with his glove. I grinned and nodded.

"All right, Sampson Park, down on the bench," Mr. Stillwell boomed out. "We're not gonna default this game, thanks to Henry, and so we're gonna win it. Right?"

"Right," we said.

"Okay. Here's our batting order. Rachel, you're up first. Take a pitch. Carter was wild last year. He'll probably be wild this year. Make him throw one strike before you start swinging. There'll be two signals from the third-base coaching box. This is the take signal."

He touched both elbows and then the peak of his cap.

"I might be giving fake signals, but that one will

be to take the next pitch. You'll always get that if the count's 3 and 0. Got it?"

"Two elbows and you touch the peak of the cap," I said. "That's take the pitch."

"For Pete's sake, Henry," Ed Godfrey said. "Why announce it to them?"

Mr. Stillwell laughed. "They're warming up. They didn't hear it. But Ed's right, Henry, it doesn't pay to talk too loudly," he said, his voice booming out.

"Yes, sir." I didn't smile. I felt good. I wished my whole family could see me now.

"Bunt is the other signal to look for. That will be when I touch both elbows and then my nose and then the peak of the cap. Any questions on the signals?"

There were none.

"Okay. Tony bats second. Gary, you're hitting in the third spot. Then Casey in cleanup. Kevin, you're number five. Mike Kohn, number six. Godfrey, seven. Ted Kohn, eight." He looked at me. "Henry, you'll be batting ninth. Have you been playing ball at all?"

"Yes, sir," I said. "I play every day."

They all looked at me, surprised. I blushed.

Dummy! Now you'll have to tell them what you do in the driveway.

But Mr. Stillwell was no fool. He could tell I was sorry I'd shot my mouth off. He didn't ask me any more questions.

"Good. Now listen up, kids. We can beat these guys if we don't beat ourselves. I'm pitching Gary for three innings, then Rachel will go two. This is only gonna be a five-inning game. Okay, Rache, get up there and make him throw at least one strike. And look for the bunt signal. You'll get it if their third baseman is playing deep."

Rachel snapped a bubble and headed for the batter's box. Mr. Stillwell headed for the third-base coaching box. Tony Greene, who was up second, slipped a doughnut over his bat and started practice swinging.

"Batter up," Jimmy the ump squeaked.

"Give it a ride," Mr. Stillwell boomed out from the third-base coaching box. This after he had privately told Rachel not to swing. That was kind of clever, I thought. I've got to remember that for my make-believe games.

Rachel stepped into the batter's box, and our bench erupted with noise.

· 25 ·

"No pitcher, Rache."

"Picking peaches, Rache."

Their team talked it up too.

"Girls can't hit," their second baseman yelled.

"Better than you," I shouted back.

Gary Stillwell looked at me and laughed. "Thatta boy, Henry."

I wished he'd call me Smitty. "Henry" just didn't sound like a ball player. Unless you were Henry Aaron who broke Babe Ruth's record. And then he was called "Hank."

I shouted lots of stuff though. Like: "Make 'em pitch to you, Rache," "He's scared of you, Rache," "He's a humpty-dumpty, Rache." (I read that one in a sports magazine.)

Maybe I wasn't such a good athlete, but I was good with words. I get A's in school. And this was fun. Sitting on the bench again with the guys. Being part of a real team again. I was kind of glad Mrs. Harrington had come to our house. This really was better than make-believe ball.

At least it was till the top of the next inning.

3

Although Rachel worked Tom Carter, their pitcher, for a walk, we didn't get any runs that inning because Tony forced her at second for our first out. Then Gary lined out to left, and Casey flied out to center field.

As I trotted out to right field, I was thinking that Carter didn't look all that fast and maybe even I could get a piece of the ball. Or crouch and work him for a walk.

After I got on, I'd take a big lead off first and draw a wild throw and hop it to second, and all the guys and Mr. Stillwell would call out: "Way to go, Smitty."

"Batter up," the umpire squeaked, and I paid attention to the real game.

Their number-four hitter was their first baseman, Michael Phelps, and he was a lefty. Ted shifted automatically toward right field. Rachel at shortstop moved toward second, and at first base Kevin Kline instinctively moved back.

Which was silly, since the right-handed hitters were not getting around on Gary's fastball and there was no reason to think the lefties would. But everyone always automatically shifts for a left-handed hitter.

In left field, Mike Kohn shouted: "Hey, Mr. Stillwell, do you want me to switch fields with Henry?"

"No, you stay right where you are, Mike," Mr. Stillwell boomed. "Pitch away," he yelled to his son, Gary.

Which was his way of telling Gary to keep on throwing hard stuff. And Gary did. He got a quick strike on Michael Phelps, then a ball, then another ball, then a strike, then a ball . . . and then Phelps started fouling off pitches.

I thought to myself: If I were pitching, I'd take something off the fastball. The guy has good wrists, good bat control, he's setting up for the fastball. He's starting to time it.

I'd give him the big motion and then throw a change-up. On 3 and 2. He'd never expect it. He'd be way out ahead of it. He'd miss it. And Phelps did. He was way out ahead of the ball. He swung and missed it by a foot and almost fell down in the batter's box.

"Way to go, Smitty," the guys behind me yelled as they whipped the ball around the infield.

Old Case made an approving fist at me.

"That's using the old noodle, Smitty," Mr. Still-well yelled.

"Good pitch, Smitty," Rachel called.

"Lucky," their third-base coach said.

"Henry!" Tony Greene screamed at me.

I blinked. Michael Phelps was running to first. He'd hit the ball somewhere. Kevin Kline was looking up at the sky.

"All yours, Henry," Mr. Stillwell's big voice was booming frantically.

Yes, all mine. But where was it? I stepped back, then in, then back, and then *crash, bam*, pain, and down I went.

I heard shouts from far away. "All the way, Mike. . . ."

I heard footsteps on the ground. Ted Kohn grunting. He was chasing the ball.

Cheers. Groans. And the earth pounded more in my ear. People were running to me. I couldn't see them. I couldn't see anyone. My head was throbbing. Everything was dark.

"Stand back, boys," Mr. Stillwell shouted. "Give Henry air."

"His glasses are broken," someone said.

"That's the least of it," someone else said.

"His father's a doctor, Mr. Stillwell."

"Henry, can you hear me? It's Mr. Stillwell. If you can hear me, open your eyes."

I opened my eyes. Mr. Stillwell's face was a blur, just inches away. Slowly, his features swam into focus. He looked scared. Beyond him I could see Jimmy the ump also looking scared, and the bases ump looking scared, and the other coach and all the kids from both teams. Everyone looked scared.

"He could have a concussion," Mike Kohn said.

"Henry, can you talk?" Mr. Stillwell yelled.

"Yes. I think so."

He looked relieved.

"Henry can always talk," Kevin Kline muttered. "That's what he was doing when Phelps hit the ball. Talking to himself. I could hear him from first base."

"I could hear him from second," Tony Greene said.

"It's my fault, Henry," Gary Stillwell said. "I threw a dumb pitch. A change-up. Phelps'd never a gotten around on a fastball."

I looked at Gary and tried to smile. I hated for Gary to feel bad. "No, I threw it too, Gary. It was the right pitch to throw."

Mr. Stillwell frowned. He thought it was a strange thing to say. He held three big fingers in front of my nose. "How many fingers am I holding up, Henry?"

"Three."

"What's the day today?"

"Saturday."

"Do you know what happened to you just now?"

"A fly ball hit me on the head."

Mr. Stillwell stood up. "I think he's all right."

"He's got a big bump on his head," someone said.

"It'll improve his looks," Ed Godfrey said.

"All right, Henry," Mr. Stillwell said, "sit up. But sit up slowly."

I sat up slowly.

"How do you feel, lad?"

"Fine."

"Woozy?"

"No, sir."

"Headache? Nausea?"

"No, sir."

"Can you stand up?"

He held his hand out, and I took it and got to my feet.

"How does that feel?"

"Okay."

"Is anyone home in your house?"

"My mother."

"I'm going to take you there right now."

"I'm all right, Mr. Stillwell. I can play."

"That's a matter of opinion," Kevin Kline said.

"Another day, Henry," Mr. Stillwell said.

"Another team, too," Ed Godfrey muttered.

"I've got to play, Mr. Stillwell. You'll default with only eight players."

"It'll be a closer game if we default," Tony Greene said.

"Let's have none of that," Mr. Stillwell growled. "Henry did his best out here."

"Here are your glasses, Henry," Rachel said. "The frame's bent."

"That's okay. Thanks, Rache."

They slid down my nose. A couple of kids laughed. I knew I looked funny.

"Here's your glove, Henry," Casey Prince said.

"Thanks, Casey."

"Ump," Mr. Stillwell said, "I guess that's the game. There's not much chance of another kid showing up now. And I don't want to take a chance with the boy's health."

"You know I don't like winning this way, Frank," the other coach said.

"I know that, Dick. I'm sorry we couldn't field a full team. Sampson Park Tigers," Mr. Stillwell's voice boomed out, "we'll stick here for some practice."

"We could play an unofficial game," the other coach said.

"That's better than nothing," Mr. Stillwell said, forcing a smile to his face.

"You'll have to do it without umps," Jimmy the ump said.

"That's all right, Jim," Mr. Stillwell boomed. "Just leave us the bases. I'll get them back to the Rec Department after the game. Henry, you still live on Colton Lane, don't ya?"

"Yes, sir, but I feel fine. I could stay and play."

"No way, lad. Not after that knock on the head. You ought to be watched. Give me five minutes to run the boy home, Dick. Let's go, Henry."

It was embarrassing . . . leaving, with everyone watching.

"So long, Henry," Rachel said.

"Take it easy, Henry," Casey said.

"You made a good try for the ball, Henry," Gary called after me. No one else said a thing.

Mr. Stillwell held on to my arm as we walked to his pickup truck.

"You mustn't feel bad about this, Henry. It can happen to the best of them. Even major leaguers get hit on the head by balls they've lost in the sun."

I stared at him. Did he really think that? Or was he offering me an excuse? I hesitated and then I shook my head. "I didn't lose it in the sun, Mr. Stillwell. I wasn't paying attention."

"Oh."

"But I might've lost it in the sun if I was paying attention."

He was startled, and then he laughed. "Henry, in baseball you've got to pay attention all the time. Even when you're not in the action. Because you could be at any second."

We turned left on Granger, crossed the intersection, and pulled up in front of our house. Mrs. Harrington's Cadillac was still in our driveway.

"Is that your Cadillac?"

"It's one of my mom's customers."

"Then I won't go in. But you tell her what happened, and that I think she and your dad ought to keep a close eye on you for the next twenty-four hours. You could have a slight concussion."

"What's a concussion, Mr. Stillwell?"

It was a word I'd used too, but I didn't exactly know what it meant.

"It's a swelling inside your head."

"I don't have that. I've got a bump on the outside."

He laughed. "Show her that then."

"I will."

As soon as Mom sees that bump, she'll never make me play real baseball again. Some good could come out of this embarrassing event.

4

Mom and Mrs. Harrington were still drinking tea. Melissa was at the table with them, reading scripts from her theater stuff. She looked at me.

"What happened to your glasses?"

All they cared about in this family were *things*.

"I got hurt." I sailed my glove over a tiger's head and onto an Asian folk-art stool.

"Henry!" Mom exclaimed. Not seeing me, just my glove sailing over her art collection.

"Where did you get hurt, Henry?" Mrs. Harrington asked.

"On my head. I have a big bump."

"That big bump is your nose," Melissa said.

"Oh, is it? Does this look like my nose?"

I bent over so she could see my forehead.

"Oh, my goodness," Mrs. Harrington said, "that is a big bump."

"I told you," I said to Melissa.

"His glasses are broken too, Mom," Melissa said. But Mom didn't care about my glasses. She even didn't care about her art collection. She was feeling the bump on my forehead.

"Ouch. That hurts."

"What happened?"

I took a deep breath. "I got into a game with my old team, the Sampson Park Tigers. I was playing second base. There was a ground ball and a runner going to second. I dove for the ball and collided with the runner. A guy named Michael Phelps. He goes to Angell School. I caught the ball and tagged him, but . . ." I shrugged.

"We better put some ice on it right away," Mom said. She'd stopped listening to me halfway through my recital.

"Well, Emily, I'll leave you to look after your wounded child. I'm sure he'll be all right. About the elephant . . ."

"Larry and I will bring it over after dinner," Mom said, going to the refrigerator and getting out a tray of ice. "Melissa, will you see Mrs. Harrington to the door?"

"Thank you, Melissa, but I'm not such an old crock that I can't see myself to the door."

"Sit down, Henry," Mom said. "Take off your glasses."

"I don't want ice."

"It will help keep the swelling down." She put about six ice cubes in a dish towel and pressed it against my forehead.

"Ouch."

"I'm not hurting you."

"Yes, you are."

"Tell us what really happened, Henry," Melissa said. "You bumped into a telephone pole, didn't you?"

"You're funny. I told you how it happened. In a baseball game."

"Here, you hold the ice, Henry."

"Where are you going?"

"To call your father. I think he ought to look at it."

"Mom, I'm all right."

But she was already calling him.

"Have no fear, brother dear, she'll never get hold of him. He's probably operating. Can you read while you hold that ice?"

"Read what?"

"The script for this play. I'm trying out for the queen in *The Princess Who Wouldn't Talk*. I need someone to feed me lines."

"Feed you lines?"

"Read the line before mine, stupid."

"You call me stupid and I won't read anything."

"Sorry. You're not stupid. Here, you be the king. I'm the queen. You start right here. 'I wonder what's ailing our daughter.' Okay?"

"You just said it. Why do you want me to say it?"

"Because it's dialogue. It's a play. And that's what will happen at the auditions on Wednesday. Someone's going to read the king while I read the queen. So I'm asking you to help me rehearse it!"

"My bump hurts."

"This will make you forget about it. Read!"

I read: *I wonder what's ailing our daughter.*

"Can't you sound more kingly?"

"I've never been a king and I don't feel so good."

"All right, read it again."

I read the line again. Just as badly.

Melissa read her lines in a phony queenly voice: *I think we have a stubborn girl on our hands. I think she enjoys being sick.*

I'm angry, I read. *No one should enjoy being sick.* The ice felt so cold. I couldn't hold it there much longer.

"Try to sound a little angry, Henry." She read: *I think we've got to send for more doctors.*

"We don't need more doctors," Mom said, coming back into the dining room. "All we need is one doctor, your father, but we can never find him. How does it feel, Henry?"

"The ice hurts more than the bump."

"Just keep holding it as long as you can. Melissa, I want you to sit here with Henry tonight after supper while your father and I take the elephant over to Mrs. Harrington's."

"I don't need a baby-sitter. I can take care of myself better than Melissa can take care of me."

"It's not just you, Henry. I have a lot of valuable things here now."

"I can call nine-one-one just as fast as she can."

"All right," Mom said. "We'll discuss it later. For all I know your father will want to take you to the hospital and get your head x-rayed."

"I don't want my head x-rayed," I said angrily.

"Now you're angry," Melissa said. "Read the line that way, Henry."

My sister has a one-track mind. I read in an angry voice: *I'm angry. No one should enjoy being sick!*

"You sound angry but not kingly."

There was no satisfying her.

Mom took the dish towel and ice from me and examined the bump.

"It doesn't look any worse," she said. "How does it feel?"

"It still hurts."

"Keep holding it."

I held the ice, and without thinking if I was supposed to or not, I read the next line in the play. It belonged to a guard.

Your Majesty, there's a young man here who says he can make the princess talk.

What's his name? I read, changing my voice from guard to king.

Jack. Jack Deakins.

Well, send him in. We need help.

Okay, Jack, I read as the guard. *You can go in now.*

Thanks, I read as Jack. Changing my voice a third time: *Who do I bow to first? The king or the queen?*

"Listen to him, Mom," Melissa said, laughing. Mom was putting the teacups and saucers into the dishwasher. "He's playing everybody at once."

"Well, he's had a lot of practice playing make-believe baseball."

"At least I don't get hurt when I play make-believe baseball."

"That's true. You better stay away from the park for a while."

Finally, I thought.

Melissa read: *I like the looks of this Jack, my dear.*

I read in what I thought was a kingly voice: *He looks rather young to me.*

"That's still not very kingly," Melissa said.

I changed my voice to Jack's. *I'm not that young. My name's Jack. Jack Deakins, and I'm not afraid of anything.*

"You do Jack a lot better than the king. The trouble is we have a Jack already."

"I'm not interested in trying out for a part in your play, Mel. Do you want to rehearse or not?"

"Rehearse."

She read the queen. And I read the king, the guard, and Jack. It was kind of fun reading all those parts. Doing it, I forgot about the bump that was hurting me and the ice that was freezing me.

5

My dad is the busiest man I know. He leaves our house at six thirty A.M. every day and sometimes doesn't come back till after Melissa and I are asleep.

It's not that he doesn't love his family. He does. But he also loves his work. Curing people.

But he couldn't have had too many sick people today, because he got home for supper while we were still on dessert. We heard him come up the walk from the garage. He was whistling cheerfully.

"Sounds like he cured someone," I said.

"It's about time," Melissa said.

"I heard that," Dad said with a laugh.

Melissa ran to him and kissed him. "Mom sold the big elephant to Mrs. Harrington."

"Did you, Em?"

"I did," Mom said proudly.

Dad kissed her. "How about that?"

"And I've got a big bump on my head," I said.

"Do you?" Dad came over to me. I was still at the table. "So you do. Did you hit your little brother with some folk art, Mel?"

Melissa laughed. "No. He played in a real baseball game for a change."

"Is that right?" Dad asked, touching my bump and around it. His fingers were strong and gentle at the same time. "Well, that's what happens sometimes when you leave the world of make-believe. You bump into real life."

"I called you about it," Mom said. "But as usual, you couldn't be reached."

"Guy Cardwell came in with cardiac arrest."

"Oh dear, how is he?"

"All right for the moment." Dad's fingers kept poking around my head. "Another thing that took up some time today was your folk art collection, Em. That hurt?"

"Just a teeny bit."

"Hurt here?"

"No."

"That's good."

"What do you mean my art collection took up your time?"

"Well, I'd been wondering for some time if we shouldn't increase our homeowner's insurance policy because of it. Then after that newspaper article came out, I knew we should. How about here, Henry?" His strong and gentle fingers were now pressing on the back of my skull. "Does that hurt?"

"No," I said.

"Good." He took his hands from my head and looked into my eyes.

"What does the newspaper story have to do with increasing our insurance, Larry?"

"Burglars read newspapers, Em. Anyway, someone from the insurance company is going to call you Monday about the value of your collection. Do you have a headache, Henry?"

"No."

"Feel nauseous?"

"No."

"How about when you were back on the field? Did you feel nauseous then?"

"No. Mr. Stillwell asked me that too. He thought I might have a concussion."

"Do you think we should have him x-rayed, Larry?"

"No. I'm pretty sure he's all right. What did you get hit with, Henry?"

"A fly ball." I didn't for a second think of making up a story for Dad.

"Wait a second," Melissa said. "You told us that you collided with someone."

"Well, that happened too."

Dad laughed. "He collided with a fly ball. What's for supper, Em?"

"Chicken, and yours is cold. I'll warm it up—"

"He can't tell the truth for two straight minutes," Melissa said.

"—but you'll have to eat quickly, Larry. I promised Mrs. Harrington you'd help me carry the elephant over to her house."

"Can't, Em. Have to be back at the hospital to look at Guy Cardwell."

"Larry, this is Saturday night. Do you have to go back to the hospital tonight?"

"Yes."

"I thought Guy was Joe Gedney's patient."

"He is, but Joe's on vacation."

"Why do *you* have to cover for him?"

"Because Joe looks after my patients when we go on vacation."

"I can help you carry the elephant, Mom," Melissa said.

"I can too," I put in.

Dad spooned a chunk of grapefruit into his mouth. "I don't think carrying elephants is prescribed for a boy who got hit on the head with a fly ball. Did you lose it in the sun?"

I shook my head. Unbelievable. Dad asked the same questions Mr. Stillwell did. Mr. Stillwell could be a doctor and Dad could be a coach. Though Dad would have to develop Mr. Stillwell's booming voice. Dad's voice was more sharp. Like a knife. Well, he was a surgeon. It all fit.

"I can't leave Henry here alone, Larry. Someone probably should keep an eye on him."

"I can keep an eye on myself."

Dad looked at me. He was pleased that I was seeming to be strong and tough. "I'll be back within the hour, Em. Henry will be okay till then. Besides, Henry, you have my number at the hospital."

"Henry bent his glasses frame too," Melissa said helpfully.

"I see that," Dad said. "They're easily fixed. Were you daydreaming, Henry?"

I nodded.

"Nothing good comes out of daydreaming, son. Making up stuff is okay if you're *not* engaged in real life. If you're going to play make-believe in real life, then you better not leave the house. You'll be safe here."

He said it like a doctor. Kingly. And I believed him.

I shouldn't have.

6

I was glad when they all left: Dad to the hospital, Mom and Melissa to deliver the elephant.

I like being alone. I know you're not supposed to like being alone. You're supposed to be lonely when you're alone. But I'm not.

When I'm alone is when I can make up stuff best. It's hard to do that with people around.

I went upstairs to my room and lay down on the bed, and even though I didn't want to, I relived the awful scene on the diamond. The fly ball. Tony Greene shouting at me. And then *bam*.

I felt the bump on my forehead. It throbbed but it didn't hurt.

All in all, the Sampson Park Tigers had been pretty nice to me considering that I'd lost the game for them. Kevin Kline was right. A tree could play better in the outfield than me.

How could a tree play better than me?

I closed my eyes.

Well, for one thing, a fly ball could hit the top of a tree and then like a marble in a pinball machine drop slowly down from branch to branch. At the same time, a fast center fielder could come running over, dive, and catch the ball before it hit the ground.

Believe it or not, that's just what happened. Gary was pitching and a kid on the Angell School Comets hit a towering fly to right field. Once again we were shorthanded, playing without a right fielder. I was in center field this time. The ball hit this big oak tree and started falling down through leaves and twigs and branches. Down, down it kept dropping. Like a marble. I ran hard, never taking my eye off it. It was just about a foot above the ground when I dove and caught it in the webbing of my glove.

"Out!" yelled the ump. It was Jimmy with the high squeaky voice.

"Way to go, Smitty," Rachel yelled.

"Great catch, Smitty," Gary and Casey shouted.

Even Kevin Kline gave me a thumbs-up signal. That was the third out, and we started to run in when the other coach came charging onto the field followed by his whole team. He yelled at Jimmy the ump that the tree was out of play. That it really should be a dead ball.

Mr. Stillwell ran over and boomed out in his big voice that the tree was in play. Soon everyone was milling about under the oak tree arguing: umps, players, coaches.

"Smitty caught it fair and square," Mr. Stillwell boomed. "How can the tree be out of play when it's in fair territory? Think of the tree like the right field wall in Tiger Stadium."

"If it's like the right field wall in Tiger Stadium, Frank, then the ball's still in play." I imitated the other coach too.

"I'm changing my call," Jimmy the ump yelled. "The tree is like a wall. They're both made of wood."

That got a good laugh from everyone except Mr. Stillwell. I opened my eyes.

The phone was ringing. Darn it. What a rotten time for that to happen. I was making up a great game. It would be hard to get back to it.

I picked up the hall phone.

"Hello."

"Henry?"

"Yes."

"It's Kevin. Kevin Kline."

Kevin had never called me before in my life.

"Oh. Hi, Kevin." Why would he call me? He didn't like me at all.

His voice was friendly, though. "How're you feeling, man?"

"Okay," I said cautiously.

"Did you get a concussion?"

"No."

"Oh." He sounded a little disappointed.

"Tony's here with me. So's Ed Godfrey. Did you . . . uh . . . get a call from Mr. Stillwell?"

"No."

"Well, uh . . ." He sounded embarrassed. "He's . . . uh . . . gonna call you. Gary told us he was."

"What about?"

"He . . . uh . . . is gonna ask you to come to our game Monday."

"Really?" I couldn't believe it.

"Yeah." Kevin hesitated. "Gary says he feels bad about your getting hurt and thinks you deserve another chance. He thinks maybe if he played you in the infield, you know, maybe you'd do better."

"I don't think I would," I said.

"We don't think so either," Kevin said, relieved that I'd said it first. "That's why I'm calling you, Henry. You're still on the roster, and if you come to the game, Mr. Stillwell's got to play you for at least an inning, and . . . well, you know. . . ."

"I know. I'll make you guys lose again."

"Right. So we were thinkin' you could tell him for the good of the team that you don't want to play this year."

"I don't."

"Great. I told the guys I knew you'd understand. Well, see you around, Henry."

"See you, Kevin."

I hung up. I lay down on my bed again. I didn't feel like going back to my make-believe game.

All baseball seemed silly. I ought to go down and watch TV. Get something to eat.

The phone rang again. I let it ring and ring. It was probably going to be Mr. Stillwell. I picked it up on the sixth ring.

"Henry, this is Mr. Stillwell." His voice boomed into my ear.

"Hi, I—"

I was going to say I know why you're calling, but I never got that far.

"Henry, are you all right?" I held the receiver away from my ear. You could puncture an eardrum listening to Mr. Stillwell.

"Yes, sir."

"The phone rang and rang. Who's home with you?"

"No one. I'm okay, Mr. Stillwell. My dad examined me and said I was okay. They'll all be back soon."

"No nausea? Headaches?"

"No, sir."

"That's good. I was worried about you. So was Gary."

"Thank you. It was nice of you. I guess you had to default."

"We did. And then we played an unofficial game and beat them with eight players. It's just too bad that league rules won't let you go past the second inning with less than nine players. The default goes into the record book as a one-to-nothing loss."

"I'm sorry, Mr. Stillwell."

"Heck, Henry, it wasn't your fault. We would have had to default if you hadn't showed up. But we get another crack at them Monday. Same team. Angell School. Do you think you can make it?"

I was silent. Mr. Stillwell plunged right on. He thought I was surprised to be asked back. I would have been if Kevin hadn't called.

"I've been thinking you might do better in the infield, Henry. At second base. We could play Tony in the outfield."

Was that one of the reasons Tony was with Kevin when he called me a minute ago?

"How does that strike you, Henry?"

"Uh . . . Mr. Stillwell, I . . . uh . . . don't think I should play this year either."

"Why not, Henry?"

What a question. " 'Cause I'm no good, Mr. Stillwell."

"You won't get better by not playing."

"I can practice at home. Alone."

"It's not the same thing. It's not the same game. I've talked with Gary and Casey and Rachel, and they think you should be a sub at least."

Tears came into my eyes.

"You wouldn't start, but you could get in for an inning. Maybe two."

"Thanks, Mr. Stillwell, but I think I'd still hurt the team. If you don't have enough players and need someone so you don't forfeit, I guess I could come down, but . . ."

"I never thought of you as a quitter, Henry."

Now I really felt awful. But I'd given my word to Kevin. "Thanks, Mr. Stillwell. Thanks . . . for calling."

"I won't take your no for a final answer. You think about it, Henry. Good night, lad."

"Good night, Mr. Stillwell."

I hung up. I felt shaky. He was a nice man. Even with his booming bellowing voice. He looked like he was one of those father-coaches who had to win at all costs. But he wasn't like that at all. He was willing to have me on the team.

I lay back down on my bed. Was I doing the

right thing in saying no? Did Gary and Casey and Rachel really want me to play? Or were they just being nice?

I closed my eyes. I wished I could do something wonderful for those guys. Win a ball game for them. Suppose the rule was that you *could* play after the second inning with less than nine players.

And suppose Mr. Stillwell put me in center field.

"Henry," he said in his deep voice, "you'll have to cover right field too. Look out for that oak tree."

Which was just where I'd been in my make-believe ball game before the phone calls threw me off the track. I had just caught a ball that had fallen through the tree, and the coaches were arguing. Each of them was yelling at Jimmy the squeaky-voiced ump.

"How're you rulin' it, Jim?" Mr. Stillwell boomed out.

Jim squeaked, "I'm rulin' it a fair ball, Coach. It's like you said, Smitty caught it off the wall."

Which means, I thought, the ball's still in play and the batter's not yet out. The kid who had hit the ball was standing there under the tree arguing like everyone else. I ran over and tagged him.

"Out!" Jim stuck his thumb up.

"What do you mean, 'out'?" their coach yelled. "Time was called."

"Who called it?" Mr. Stillwell bellowed. "I didn't hear anyone call 'Time.' Quick thinking, Smitty."

Everyone pounded me on the back as we ran in for our at bat.

"Man," said Kevin Kline, "that was fast thinking."

"You're up first, Smitty," Mr. Stillwell called out. "Give it a ride."

I stepped into the batter's box.

Their pitcher made a big show out of rubbing the ball. Then he double pumped and fired. I looked that ball right into my bat. I swung and connected. Right on the nose. Shouts went up. The ball was going out. It was carrying all the way to the Junior Theater building.

Oh no, I thought, rounding first, watching the ball descend. It was going to hit a window.

There was a sharp crack of glass. Only, curiously, it seemed to come before the ball hit. And then more glass broke. And still more glass. Like little broken pieces were being pushed in. And then there was a thud and another thud. And then I came wide awake and alert.

Those noises were coming from downstairs. The breaking glass sounds had not come from a make-believe ball game. They had come from the glass door to the patio. Someone was breaking into our house.

I lay there, my eyes wide open, my heart pounding.

7

Every month the *Arborville News* runs what it calls a "crime map." It's a map that shows where burglaries or attempted burglaries have taken place the previous month. Solid blue dots stand for burglaries; blue circles stand for burglary attempts.

Mom and Dad always look at the map closely and say: "Hmm . . . none in our neighborhood." Or: "There was a burglary attempt over on Lincoln Avenue [two blocks away]. I wonder whose house it was."

And now we were going to be a solid blue dot or a blue circle.

I got up from the bed and tiptoed to the door. They had turned off the lights. A flashlight beam played around the living room. "Get that," a man whispered.

They were stealing Mom's Asian folk art.

"And that," the robber said.

I can't let them do it, I thought. My mind raced into an idea.

I bellowed out in Mr. Stillwell's voice: "Larry, there's someone down there. Get your shotgun."

Then I slammed my door and opened it again and shouted back in Dad's sharp voice: "I got it, Frank. You grab my kid's Louisville Slugger."

"I got it," Mr. Stillwell boomed.

"Then let's get 'em," Dad yelled.

I started running in place, coming down as hard as I could. I slammed my door open and shut and boomed out in Mr. Stillwell's voice: "This way, Larry!"

I was making such a racket I couldn't hear a thing from downstairs. For all I knew they were charging up the stairs right now, guns in their hands.

But then, over my racket, I heard the most beautiful sound in the world: the sound of a car

starting in our driveway. I ran to the window. A van, without lights, squealed its tires as it shot out of our driveway. It roared off down the street and passed under the streetlight. It had a white stripe in back.

I almost sank to the floor with relief. But it wasn't over yet. I ran to the hall phone and punched 911. My throat felt dry.

"Nine-one-one operator," a voice on the phone said.

Without thinking, I spoke in Dad's voice. "This is Dr. Larry Smith, Fourteen eleven Colton Lane, off Granger and Ferdon. Two burglars just broke into my house. I scared them off. They're in a van with a white stripe in the back. Driving up Hermitage Road. Without lights."

I paused. I didn't know what else to say.

"Does anyone require an ambulance?" the 911 voice asked.

"No, I'm all right," I said. And then I started to cry. Out of nowhere I cried. And in my own voice, my ten-year-old voice, I said, "I'm all right."

Silence. And then: "Sit tight, whoever you are. I'll have a police car out there right away."

I sat down on the floor. I was shaking like a leaf. I hadn't known how scared I was till I phoned 911.

It may have been all of five minutes before I heard noises outside, a car, and then flashing red lights reflected red on the walls and ceiling.

There was a banging at the front door and at the side door, and then flashlight beams played inside the dark living room, and then all the doors opened at once and there were shouts and voices and all the lights came on at once.

Looking down the stairs, I could see two policemen with guns in their hands.

"Police!" one of them shouted.

And then they both whirled about pointing their guns toward the kitchen.

"What's going on?" I heard Dad's voice. He must have just come in the side door. "I live here."

"What's your name?" a policeman asked.

"Larry Smith."

"He's the one who called in the burglary."

"I didn't call in anything. I was at the hosp— Wait a second."

Dad raced up the stairs. In a flash he was bending over me. "Henry, are you all right? What happened? Look at me, son."

"Looks like they hit him on the head," one of the policemen said.

I looked up at Dad.

"They didn't do that. Henry, are you all right?"

I nodded. I couldn't speak.

He picked me up and carried me into my room and laid me down on the bed.

"Did you see the burglars, son?" one of the cops asked.

I shook my head. Dad was quietly checking me over for bruises other than the one on my forehead.

"If you didn't call the police, mister, who did?"

The radio in the police car outside burst into sound. The second policeman ran down the stairs.

"I did," I said. Slowly the trembles were going out of me.

"Did you say you were me, Henry?"

"Yes."

I sat up.

The second cop came back up the stairs. "Car two-oh-two stopped the van on Washtenaw.

Two suspects. They're bringing them over here now."

"He didn't see them," Dad said. "He won't be able to identify them."

Dad was scared for me. He wanted to protect me.

"That's okay," the first cop said. "We'll be able to match tire tracks. Someone burned a lot of rubber leaving your driveway. Something here sure scared them."

"I did."

They stared at me.

"All right, Henry," Dad said gently, "tell us what happened."

I took a deep breath and told Dad and the two policemen everything that had happened. From after the phone call from Mr. Stillwell, and I was playing my make-believe baseball game again and had hit a home run, only it wasn't the glass in Junior Theater that broke but the glass patio door downstairs, and I realized there were burglars in the house.

"I didn't want to let them rob Mom's art, Dad."

"What did you do, Henry?"

"I pretended I was Mr. Stillwell—he's my baseball coach. He shouts a lot. I imitated him yelling at Dad to get his shotgun. And he got a baseball bat. I imitated Dad and jumped up and down and slammed the door. That's what I did."

The cops listened politely. But I could tell they didn't believe me.

Dad's face was grave. "Let's hear how you did it, Henry. How you imitated me and Mr. Stillwell. Can you stand up and do it?"

Later I thought Dad was also being a doctor. Getting me back to normal. It was the right thing to do. All the fear and shakes left me as I imitated Mr. Stillwell's booming voice and Dad's sharper one and yelled about a shotgun and a Louisville Slugger. I ran up and down and banged the door open and shut.

The policemen were flabbergasted.

But I still don't think they believed me until a third policeman came into the house.

"The tire tracks match," he called up the stairs. "We also found some loot in the van from two other burglaries in this neighborhood. One of the suspects said they left this place because there were two men in the house, and one had a shotgun and the other a baseball bat."

Silence. And then one of our policemen shook his head and said, "Well, that answers that, doesn't it?"

The other said to Dad, "You got one cool kid there, mister."

"I think so too," Dad said. He turned to me. "But why did you pretend to be me when you called nine-one-one?"

"I don't know."

"He probably thought we'd get here faster," a policeman said.

"He's right," the other said.

"*Do* you have a shotgun, Dr. Smith?" the first policeman asked.

"No," Dad said. "We don't have any guns."

"You probably don't need any with a kid like this around."

After that the policemen went outside, where a crowd of neighbors had gathered and where more police and detectives were gathered around the van with the two suspects.

I was glad I didn't have to confront the suspects. I think I would have been scared all over again. I don't know if they were told the truth then and there about the two adults, the shotgun, and the baseball bat. I was just glad they were taken away.

One of our neighbors helped Dad board up the broken patio door.

And finally, Dad and I were alone.

We looked at each other. Dad shook his head and smiled. "Henry, I owe you an apology. I'll never knock make-believe again. Especially in real life."

"I lost the game for Sampson Park because of it, Dad."

"You certainly saved us here tonight, though."

"Mom and Melissa will never believe it."

"They will when they see the broken door."

But they didn't believe it, because when they came home and Mom saw the broken patio door, she said: "Henry! You've been playing inside the house again. I told you—"

Dad laughed. "Em, Henry didn't break that door. A couple of burglars did. But one of Henry's make-believe games saved your art collection from being stolen."

"What are you talking about?"

"Tell them, Henry. Tell them what happened."

I told them.

"I don't believe it," Melissa said. "I think Henry

made all that up because he broke the door. And maybe you were playing make-believe baseball or football with him, Dad."

Aren't big sisters tough?

"Is it true, Larry?" Mom asked Dad.

"Yes. We've had a busy time here tonight. And, I suspect, it will be even busier tomorrow."

I didn't know what Dad meant by that until the next day, when the phone rang and rang and people kept coming over to our house. I think all of Arborville came over.

Including the Sampson Park Tigers and Mr. Stillwell.

8

The *Arborville News* is an afternoon paper, but on Sundays it comes out in the morning. It gets delivered to our house about eight o'clock, but we don't usually look at it till about eleven.

But that Sunday morning we were awakened early by the phone ringing and people calling to tell us what they had just read.

"Go down and get the paper, Henry," Dad said after the third phone call.

I went downstairs, and there the story was. On the front page, no less.

TEN-YEAR-OLD THWARTS
BURGLARS

Henry Smith of 1411 Colton Lane pre-
vented a sure robbery at his house last night
by outwitting a pair of intruders, according
to chief of detectives Ron Keller.

"Dad," I yelled, "we *are* in the newspaper."

Mom, Dad, and Melissa came running down, and Dad read the story out loud. It told how I imitated him and "coach Frank Stillwell of the Sampson Park Tigers in the Arborville Ten-Year-Old Baseball League. In addition to his acting abilities, Henry Smith plays keen baseball for the Sampson Park Tigers."

"Oh, no, they'll think I told that to the police. I never said I was a good baseball player."

"That's a newspaper for you," Dad said. "Making a better story out of a good one."

Mom read the account again. And when she was done, she got scared. She dropped the paper and hugged me. "Henry," she said.

Melissa also read it by herself. "Well," she said when she was done, "I guess he's going to be famous now."

The phone rang. This time it was Mrs. Harrington.

"We're all right, Mrs. Harrington," Mom said. "No, they didn't get anything. Henry saved the whole collection. . . . Did he?"

Mom came back and reported that Mr. Harrington liked the elephant just as much in the daytime as he did at night. "And he and Mrs. Harrington both think Henry ought to get a medal from the president."

The phone rang again.

"How long is this going to go on?" Melissa said.

This time it was a doctor friend of Dad's. After that it was a friend of Mom's. Then two operating-room nurses called Dad to say they'd just read the paper. Then a patient of Dad's. The last straw for Melissa was when her friends started calling and asked her to get my autograph for them.

"They want his autograph," she said. "My little brother's."

"Well, your little brother is a hero," Dad said.

"I don't care. It's tiresome."

"I think we ought to leave the phone off the hook for a while," Mom said.

"Can't do that," Dad said. "I'm on call this weekend."

It wouldn't have made any difference, because right about then the doorbell started ringing. It was neighbors wanting to know where the break-in had occurred and wanting to shake my hand.

Then we got a phone call from Channel 2 in Detroit. They wanted to send a film crew over here to interview me this morning.

"No way," Dad said. "He's too young. No interviews."

The doorbell rang while Dad was arguing with the Detroit TV station.

"It's for Henry again," Melissa called.

This time it was Mr. Stillwell and the whole Sampson Park team. They were standing on our front steps. Their bikes were all over the lawn. Mr. Stillwell's pickup truck was parked out front.

Oh, boy, I thought, they're mad at me because the newspaper story said I was a keen ball player.

"Mr. Stillwell, I didn't talk to a newspaper. I just talked to the police. And I never said I was a good ball player. I just said I . . . uh . . . imitated my baseball coach."

I felt my ears burning. It's one thing to tell your father and two policemen you imitated a baseball coach; it's another thing to say it right to the coach's face.

"Nothing to be sorry about, Henry," Mr. Stillwell boomed out. He was grinning from ear to ear. "I can always use the ink. We came over to tell you that now you've *got* to play for us tomorrow."

I stared at him.

"I got a phone call this morning from Channel Seven in Detroit. They want to take pictures of you playing in a game. So Henry, you're *starting* for us tomorrow at second base. Tony's gonna play in the outfield. The whole team's excited and happy, aren't you, gang?"

If I could have taken a picture of the whole team being excited and happy, it would have won a prize. I mean: Only Rachel and Gary and Casey looked halfway happy. And they also looked halfway worried.

But Rachel winked at me and said, "Darn right, Henry."

Kevin Kline wouldn't look at me. Ed Godfrey was staring at his sneakers. Tony Greene, whose position I was taking, stood there with his arms folded. The Kohn twins looked at the sky.

Mr. Stillwell's big voice boomed. "Tomorrow there'll be media at our game." He said "media" like it was candy. He rolled it off his tongue. "We're gonna show the whole world what classy baseball is played in the Arborville Ten-Year-Old League. Right, gang?"

"Darn right," Rachel said again.

"Can't they film a practice, Mr. Stillwell?" Kevin asked.

"They want to film a game. And I told them we've got a game tomorrow." He looked back at me. "There'll be a lot of pressure on you, Henry, but nothing you can't handle. *Two* robbers you chased off. Heck, one would've scared me to death. We'll see you at Diamond One at the park at five thirty. Right?"

I gulped. And nodded. Dad came to the door to see what was going on. When he and Mr. Stillwell saw each other, they both broke into laughter.

"Well, Dr. Smith, I see Henry got you some ink too."

"Didn't he?" Dad laughed and put his arm around me.

"Your boy's a bona fide hero," Mr. Stillwell boomed. "I'm starting him at second base tomorrow night. I hope you and Mrs. Smith can come. There's gonna be a TV crew from Channel Seven filming the game."

Dad looked at me. "That'll be a lot of pressure for you, Henry."

"Dad says Smitty can handle it," Gary said.

I almost jumped out of my skin. It was the first time anyone besides me in my make-believe games had called me that.

It had sounded so natural.

"Were you scared last night, Henry?" Rachel asked.

I nodded. I guess I'd have to earn "Smitty" from the rest of them. On the field.

"Boy, you really thought fast," Casey said, grinning. "I couldn't a done it."

"Just do the same thing on the diamond, Henry," Mr. Stillwell boomed.

"You got to run, hit, and field on the diamond, not think," Kevin muttered.

"You can think in baseball too, Kevin," Mr.

Stillwell said. "Well, congratulations, Henry. And we'll see you tomorrow at five thirty."

"So long, Henry."

"Good going, Henry."

"Way to go, Henry."

They left. Dad looked at me. "That was very nice, their coming over like that."

Melissa, who had heard the whole thing, grinned at me. "Gee, Henry. Not only do you have to play real baseball now, but you've got to do it in front of millions of people. You better not get hit by a fly ball tomorrow."

"Don't tease him, Mel," Dad said. "Henry did a wonderful thing last night."

Melissa came over and gave me a hug. "I know you did. I think you were really brave, Henry. I'm proud of you too."

"Yeah, but you're right, Mel. I better not get hit by a fly ball tomorrow."

There were more phone calls, and more people came to congratulate me, but already I was beginning to worry about tomorrow. If last night had been a nightmare, tomorrow on Diamond One could be even worse.

9

Dad hit ground balls to me that afternoon in our backyard, and I fielded most of them. But I knew it would be different in a game situation.

That night I hardly slept. For one thing, the phone was still ringing. At one point a radio station in California called wanting a phone interview with me. Someone called to tell us I'd made the Associated Press wire services. All the newspapers in the country might be running the story.

The next morning reporters from the *Arborville News* and the Detroit papers came to the house. Melissa snuck me out the back door while Mom told the reporters there would be no interviews.

"Go to the police. They have all the facts," Mom told them.

While the reporters were in front talking to Mom, I got my bike out of the garage and biked out of our backyard and down to the river. I sat by the river for a long time trying to empty out my mind. But instead of getting calmer, I was becoming more nervous. If this was what being famous was like, it was a terrible thing.

I began to feel sorry for ball players like Wade Boggs and Dwight Gooden and Kirk Gibson.

When I got back, the house was empty except for Mom. Melissa was at Junior Theater. Around three o'clock Dad called to ask how I was feeling.

"Terrible," I said.

He laughed. "You'll do fine. Just concentrate. And don't play make-believe baseball while you're playing real ball."

"I know. I know."

"I'm going to do my best to make it to the game."

"Don't come. I'll feel better if you don't come."

Dad laughed.

I said the same thing to Mom.

"Nonsense," Mom said. "Of course I'll be there. I think everyone in Arborville will be there."

"What for? To see two ten-year-old teams play baseball?"

"No. They think they might be on TV."

Mom was right. The area around Diamond One was already crowded when I got there. People were sitting all over, on blankets, on chairs. There's a little bleacher that seats about forty people. There wasn't an inch of space left on it.

A white van that said Channel 7 on it was parked alongside the stands. There were TV people laying out cables, setting up lights, a microphone; a woman with a big video camera was looking at the crowd; a man carrying a battery pack was talking with people in the stands.

"Here comes our star," someone called out.

Everyone looked at me. I wished there were a hole I could have crawled into. The camera was pointed at me.

"Over here, Henry," Mr. Stillwell's voice boomed out over the others.

He was talking to a man in a white suit.

"Henry, I want you to meet Mr. Arneson, pres-

ident of the Arborville Recreational Baseball Leagues. Arne, this is Henry Smith."

Mr. Arneson had deep-blue eyes. He stuck out his hand. "Proud to meet you, Henry. You're bringing the Arborville Recreational Baseball Leagues to the attention of the world."

My knees started to shake.

"Henry, you better throw a ball around," Mr. Stillwell said, winking at me.

The Sampson Park Tigers were loosening up along the left-field foul line. To get there I had to run around the diamond, on which the Angell School Comets were having infield practice.

"There goes Henry Smith, hero," their shortstop said.

"Where's your SWAT team, Henry?" their catcher said to me.

They laughed. I ignored them.

I ran up the left-field foul line past the two umps. They were anchoring third base. One of them was our old friend Jimmy the ump.

Jimmy looked up. "Hey, congratulations, Henry," he said.

"Thanks," I said. I think he meant that.

Finally, I got to where my team was loosening up. Rachel tossed a ball at me.

"Throw easy, Henry," she said.

Throwing was probably the thing in baseball I did best. That was because of the hours I spent firing a baseball at the mattress.

"How're ya feelin', Henry?" Casey asked. He and Gary were paired off playing catch.

"Good, Casey." Why couldn't I call him "Case" the way the other kids did and the way I did in make-believe games?

"You a little scared, Henry?" Rachel asked as she tossed me one sidearm.

"A lot."

"I am too."

"I don't believe that, Rache."

"I almost threw up this afternoon."

"I hope I get a hit. I never been on TV before," Ed Godfrey said.

"They won't be taking your picture, Godfrey," Ted Kohn said.

"Yeah, it'd break the camera," Mike Kohn said.

"Funny, man."

"How many people you think are here, Case?" Gary asked.

"Lots."

"They filled the seats a half hour ago."

"That ain't so hard to do."

"Look at those girls walking back and forth in front of the camera."

"That's one way to get on TV."

"The other way's to capture two robbers."

"I didn't capture them."

"You helped, man."

"Hey, Henry, you think you'll be a cop when you grow up?"

"No."

"Here comes Ray Harvey."

Ray Harvey was on the Channel 7 news each night.

"He looks thinner than he does on TV."

"TV makes you fat, my dad says."

"Henry, he wants to interview you."

"I bet."

"He's been asking for you ever since they got here."

Ray Harvey was smiling and waving at people who were calling out his name. He came over to us.

"Which one of you is Henry?"

"Henry who?" Casey asked innocently.

Ray Harvey laughed. "C'mon. Henry Smith."

"Him," Rachel said, pointing to me.

Ray Harvey gave me an easy smile. "Henry, I'd like to ask you a few questions over by home plate, where we've got a nice background."

"No way, Ray," boomed Mr. Stillwell, coming up and taking Mr. Harvey by the arm as though they were old friends. "The lad's getting ready for a big game. But here's someone who'll give you a great interview."

Mr. Arneson stuck out his hand. "Arne Arneson. League director." He started steering the TV anchorman toward the camera behind the backstop. "Ray, I'd love to tell Channel Seven's audience about our program here in Arborville. We feel we have one of the strongest kids' baseball programs in the state."

"But—" Ray Harvey protested as he was steered away from us.

Mr. Stillwell laughed. "That's the way to throw, Henry. Nice and easy."

"I bet Henry could pitch, Mr. Stillwell," Rachel said.

"He might at that," Mr. Stillwell agreed, "but not tonight."

"I only pitch to mattresses," I said.

"Mr. Stillwell," said a high squeaky voice. Jim had come up. "Your team can take the field now."

"Thanks, Jim.

"Okay, Tigers. Gather 'round. Outfield, Gary'll hit to you. I'll hit to the infield. Ed, you're on third. Rachel short. Henry's at second. Henry, if you don't catch it cleanly, just keep it in front of you. You've got a short throw to first. Kevin, you're at first. No errors. Everyone concentrates. First catch it. *Then* throw it. Okay, kids, take the field."

"Let's go," Rachel yelled.

I felt shaky as I ran out to second base. I hoped I wouldn't trip crossing the third-base line. I didn't.

There was a lot of clapping. And I saw the TV camerawoman aim the camera at me.

"That's him," a woman said. "The kid who caught the burglars."

Now everyone was saying I'd caught them. Pretty soon it would turn out I'd tracked them down. And the truth was I hadn't even seen them.

"Play for one," Mr. Stillwell shouted.

He hit easy grounders to each of us. When my turn came, I uttered a little prayer. Please let me catch it cleanly. This is important. I've got to get off to a good start.

The crowd was silent. It was only infield practice, but everyone was watching me, including the camera. Mr. Stillwell hit me an easy grounder. I caught it and flipped it to first and breathed out.

So did everyone else on the team.

Five minutes later the game began, and in the first inning the TV crew got all the pictures they wanted and then some.

10

The Angell School Comets were up first. Gary looked nervous on the mound. He was throwing weird. Slow. Babying the ball up there. Gary threw the hardest of anyone in the ten-year-old league in Arborville.

He walked their first batter on four straight slow pitches. He threw a nice slow fat pitch to the second batter, and the guy promptly banged it into left field for a single. The runner on first stopped at second. Two men on. No one out.

Mr. Stillwell bellowed: "Gary. Don't do that. Fire away."

When Mr. Stillwell said, "Don't do that," I suddenly realized what Gary was doing. He was throwing slow pitches because he wanted them to get around on the ball and hit it to the left side . . . away from me. And it just wasn't a natural way for him to pitch.

I was embarrassed, but I didn't think anyone but me and Mr. Stillwell and Gary knew what he was doing.

Anyway, Gary started firing. He threw bullets and he threw them for strikes. He struck out their third batter on three straight pitches.

And we started hollering.

"They got holes in their bats," Rachel yelled.

"They can't see you on a Sunday," Ed Godfrey said. I didn't get that at all.

"Give 'em smoke," Kevin kept repeating. "Give 'em smoke."

Old Case behind the plate made an encouraging fist.

I didn't say anything. My throat felt dry. I didn't feel I could talk at all. The TV camera was aimed at me. They were waiting for a ball to be hit at me, and with Gary throwing bullets, someone swinging late from the right side was sure to do it.

I held my breath. The fourth batter swinging late hit a ground ball just foul past first base. Then he hit a pop-up to the right side.

"Get it," Ray Harvey shouted.

For a second I thought he was talking to me. Maybe he was. The ball was coming down between me and Kevin. I could see it but I wasn't sure I could catch it.

Kevin called me off. "I got it," he yelled, and gobbled it up.

"For Pete's sake," I heard Ray Harvey say.

I ran to second in case the runner had any ideas.

"Infield fly rule," Jimmy the ump called out. "Batter's out anyway."

Sure. I forgot about that. Someone giggled. That made it two outs. Gary looked at me worriedly. They were hitting his fastball and hitting it toward me.

"Time, ump," Rachel said, and ran into the mound. I ran in too. So did Ed and Kevin.

"Let's try a pickoff play," Rachel said. "The runner on second's taking a big lead. He's watching me, but he's not looking at Henry at all. He doesn't think Henry could catch a throw from you, Gary."

"I couldn't."

"Don't be silly. It's just like playing catch with me."

"Gary'll throw harder."

"No, I won't, Henry," Gary said.

"If you don't throw harder, you won't get him," Kevin said.

"C'mon, kids," Jimmy squeaked, "let's get the game moving. A lot of spectators are getting restless."

"We're setting up a play, ump," Rachel said.

"Listen, Henry," Gary said, "when I go to my stretch position, count one potato two and run to the bag. The ball will be there nice and easy and we'll get the guy."

"Okay," I said, though I didn't believe it.

The big crowd was getting impatient. So was Mr. Stillwell. He didn't know what was going on.

"Batter up," the plate umpire shouted.

Jimmy took his field umpiring position behind second.

Gary stepped on the rubber. He went to a

stretch position. "One potato two," I said, and cut to the bag.

"Get it," Ray Harvey called.

Gary whirled and threw. He threw a nice, easy ball. A baby could have caught it; a turtle could have outrun it. Grinning, the base runner trotted back to the bag.

I caught the ball and tagged him anyway. He laughed at me.

I said without thinking, "Out," and I said it in Jimmy's squeaky voice.

The runner turned around and yelled, "What do you mean 'out'?"

He left the bag. I tagged him again.

"*Now* you're out," Jimmy squeaked, a big grin on his face. His thumb shot upward.

For a moment no one knew what had happened except me and Jimmy. The base runner didn't even know. Their coach came out to ask what was going on.

Then Rachel got it. She chortled. She smacked me on the back. "Way to go, Henry."

She told everyone what I'd done.

Gary laughed. Casey hugged me. Tony Greene

came running in from right field and jumped on my shoulders. Kevin Kline high fived me. "That's heads-up baseball, Smitty."

I looked at him. He'd called me "Smitty."

I smiled. "No, Kev, it wasn't heads-up baseball. It was make-believe baseball."

"C'mon, Tigers, hustle in," Mr. Stillwell boomed. "The game's not over."

11

Well, my story ends here. We won the game 3–1. And I'd like to tell you I hit a home run or took part in a double play, but I didn't.

That crazy pickoff play did help take the pressure off everyone. After that play, the TV people left. They had gotten exactly what they wanted: me in action putting a tag on a runner.

We watched it that night on the news. Ray Harvey did a smooth voice-over narration. On camera, he tied it in with the robbery.

That robbery. . . . It felt as though it had happened a long time ago.

Dad never made it from the hospital to the game. Mom and Melissa gave him a blow-by-blow description. And I was so into the game, I never knew that they were there or that Dad wasn't.

After we watched the pickoff play on the news, Dad said, "Henry, it wasn't a baseball play, not really."

"I know. I didn't even do it on purpose."

"That's all to the good," Dad said. "But it does lead me to conclude that if you don't make it to the big leagues, you might have a future on Broadway."

"Speaking of which," Melissa said, "Henry, would you try out for the king in *The Princess Who Wouldn't Talk*? We haven't cast a king yet. And I think you could do it."

"Mel, I can't sound like a king. I read it the other night and you *said* I didn't sound kingly."

"That's because you don't know what a king sounds like."

"What does a king sound like?"

"Your father," Mom said, amused. "Try sounding like him."

"Now wait a second," Dad said.

"Women, my dear Emily," Mom said, "belong in the house."

I repeated it, but in Dad's voice.

"Perfect," Melissa said.

Dad shook his head. "I'm sorry I ever suggested the theater as a career for you, Henry."

I wasn't, though. On Wednesday I tried out for the part of the king and got it. Using Dad's voice all the way. Acting, it turned out, was a lot of fun. Of course I'd always been doing it. I just never thought of it as acting. Just playing make-believe.

The funny part was that now, between Junior Theater and the Sampson Park School Tigers, summer was flying by and I had no time for make-believe baseball.

But as I warned Mom, come football season, I was going to play tooken in the end zone.

"Not in the house, you won't," Mom said. "And if you have to do it outside, away from my flowers, please."

Everything had changed and nothing had changed. Mom was still dead set against make-believe ball games. That's what I thought. I was wrong.

One crisp fall afternoon I played tooken outside. I gathered in a football in the end zone next to the garage and began running it back, dodging eleven New York Giants' tackles.

The crowd rose to its feet as I faked two tacklers right into the ground. I was up to the 30-yard line already.

"All the way," they screamed.

My teammates were cheering me on from the sidelines. I leaped over one tackler and cut around another.

I crossed the 50 still going strong. Down to the 40. I raced along the sidelines. The 30 . . . the 25. . . . Only one man stood between me and the goal line, but he was their surest tackler. An all-pro.

He angled toward me. I gave him a piece of my right leg and then took it away as he dove for it. I accelerated, and with the cries of the crowd, the TV and radio announcers, my coach and teammates, ringing in my ears, I crossed the goal line. A 105-yard kickoff return!

"Touchdown!" the TV announcer yelled into his microphone.

"Touchdown!" the fans screamed.

And then a familiar voice split the air.

"Way to go, Smitty!"

It was Mom. She had both arms in the air, signaling touchdown. I laughed. And then I spiked the ball . . . away from her flowers.